THE BIRD CATCHER

The Bird Catcher

originally published
in *Museum of Horrors*
edited by Dennis Etchison
This Edition Diplodocus Press 2018

published by Diplodocus Press
Bangkok • Los Angeles

for information about the author:
www.somtow.com
about this publisher
www.diplodocuspress.com

ISBN
978-1-9409991-8-0

0 9 8 7 6 5 4 3 2 1

S.P. SOMTOW

THE BIRD CATCHER

DIPLODOCUS PRESS
BANGKOK · LOS ANGELES

THE BIRD CATCHER

THE BIRD CATCHER

There was this other boy in the internment camp. His name was Jim. After the war, he made something of a name for himself. He wrote books, even a memoir of the camp that got turned into a Spielberg movie. It didn't turn out that gloriously for me.

My grandson will never know what it's like to be consumed with hunger, hunger that is heartache. Hunger that can propel you past insanity. But I know. I've been there. So has that boy

Jim; that's why I really don't envy him his Spielberg movie.

After the war, my mother and I were stranded in China for a few more years. She was penniless, a lady journalist in a time when lady journalists only covered church bazaars, a single mother at a time when "bastard" was more than a bad word.

You might think that at least we had each other, but my mother and I never intersected. Not as mother and son, not even as Americans awash in great events and oceans of Asian faces.   We were both loners. We were both vulnerable.

That's how I became the boo-gieman's friend.

He's long dead now, but they keep him, you know, in the Museum of Horrors.   Once in a generation, I visit him.   Yesterday, I took my grandson Corey.   Just as I took his father before him.

The destination stays the same, but the road changes every generation. The first time I had gone by boat, along the quiet back canals of the old city.   Now there was an expressway. The toll was forty baht — a dollar — a month's salary that would have been, back in the 50s, in old Siam.

My son's in love with Bangkok, the insane skyline, the high tech blending with the low tech, the skyscraper shaped like a giant robot, the palatial shopping malls, the kinky sex bars, the bootleg software arcades, the whole tossed salad.   And he doesn't mind the heat. He's a big-time entrepreneur here, owns a taco chain.

I live in Manhattan. It's quieter.

I can be anonymous. I can be alone. I can nurse my hunger in secret.

Christmases, though, I go to Bangkok; this Christmas, my grandson's eleventh birthday, I told my son it was time. He nodded and told me to take the chauffeur for the day.

So, to get to the place, you zigzag through the world's raunchiest traffic, then you fly along this madcap figure-eight expressway, cross the river where stone demons stand guard on the parapets of the Temple of Dawn, and then you're suddenly in this sleazy alley. Vendors hawk bowls of soup and pickled guavas. The directions are on a handwritten placard attached to a street sign with duct tape.

It's the Police Museum, upstairs from the local morgue. One wall is covered with photographs of corpses. That's not part of the museum; it's a public service display for people with missing family members to check if any of them have turned up dead. Corey didn't pay attention to the photographs; he was busy with Pokémon.

Upstairs, the feeling changed. The stairs creaked. The upstairs room was garishly lit. Glass cases along the walls were filled with medical oddities, two-headed babies and the like, each one in a jar of formaldehyde, each one me-ticulously labeled in Thai and English. The labels weren't printed, mind you. Handwritten. There was definitely a middle school show-and-tell feel about the exhibits. No air conditioning. And no more breeze from the river like in the old days; sky-scrapers had stifled the city's breath.

There was a uniform, sick-yellow tinge to all the displays ... the neutral cream paint was edged with yellow ... the deformed livers, misshappen brains, tumorous embryos all floating in a dull yellow fluid ... the heaps of dry bones an orange-yellow, the rows of skulls yellowing in the cracks ... and then there were the young novices, shaven-headed little boys in yellow robes, staring in a heat-induced stupor as their mentor droned on about the transience of all existence, the quintessence of Buddhist philosophy.

And then there was Si Ui.

He had his own glass cabinet, like a phone booth, in the middle of the room. Naked. Desiccated. A mummy. Skinny. Mud-colored, from the embalming process, I think. A sign (handwritten, of course) explained who he was. See Ui. Devourer of children's livers in the 1950s. My grandson reads Thai more fluently than I do. He sounded out the name right away.

Si Sui Sae Ung.

"It's the boogieman, isn't it?" Corey said. But he showed little more than a passing interest. It was the year Pokémon Gold and Silver came out. So many new monsters to catch, so many names to learn.

"He hated cages," I said.

"Got him!" Corey squealed. Then, not looking up at the dead man, "I know who he was. They did a documentary on him. Can we go now?"

"Didn't your maid tell you stories at night? To frighten you? 'Be a good boy, or Si Ui will eat your liver?'"

"Gimme a break, grandpa. I'm too old for that shit." He paused. Still wouldn't look up at him. There were other glass booths in the room, other mummified criminals: a serial rapist down the way. But Si Ui was the star of the show. "Okay," Corey said, "she did try to scare me once. Well, I was like five, okay? Si Ui. You watch out, he'll eat your liver, be a good boy now. Sure, I heard that before. Well, he's not gonna eat my liver now, is he? I mean, that's probably not even him; it's probably like wax or something."

He smiled at me. The dead man did not.

"I knew him," I said. "He was my friend."

"I get it!" Corey said, back to his Gameboy. "You're like me in this Pokémon game. You caught a monster once. And tamed him. You caught the most famous monster in Thailand."

"And tamed him?" I shook my head. "No, not tamed."

"Can we go to McDonald's now?"

"You're hungry."

"I could eat the world!"

"After I tell you the whole story."

"You're gonna talk about the Chinese camp again, grandpa? And that kid Jim, and the Spielberg movie?"

"No, Corey, this is something I've never told you about before. But I'm telling you so when I'm gone, you'll know to tell your son. And your grandson."

"Okay, grandpa."

And finally, tearing himself away from the video game, he willed himself to look.

The dead man had no eyes; he could not stare back.

He hated cages. But his whole life was a long imprisonment ... without a cage, he did not even exist.

Listen, Corey. I'll tell you how I met the boogieman.

Imagine I'm eleven years old, same as you are now, running wild on a leaky ship crammed with coolies. They're packed into the lower deck. We can't afford the upper deck, but when they saw we were white, they waved us on up without checking our tickets. It looks more interesting down there. And the food's got to be better. I can smell a Chinese breakfast. That oily fried bread, so crunchy on the outside, dripping with pig fat ... yeah.

It's hot. It's boring. Mom's on the prowl. A job or a husband, whichever comes first. Everyone's fleeing the communists. We're some of the last white people to get out of China.

Someone's got a portable charcoal

stove on the lower deck, and there's a toothless old woman cooking congee, fanning the stove. A whiff of opium in the air blends with the rich gingery broth. Everyone down there's clustered around the food. Except this one man. Harmless-looking. Before the Japs came, we had a gardener who looked like that. Shirtless, thin, by the railing. Stiller than a statue. And a bird on the railing. Also unmoving. The other coolies are ridiculing him, making fun of his Hakka accent, calling him simpleton.

I watch him.

"Look at the idiot," the toothless woman says. "Hasn't said a word since we left Swatow."

The man has his arms stretched out, his hands cupped. Frozen. Concentrated. I suddenly realize I've snuck down the steps myself, pushed my through all the Chinese around the cooking pot, and I'm halfway there. Mesmerized. The man is stalking the bird, the boy stalking the man. I try not to breathe as I creep up.

He pounces. Wrings the bird's neck ... in one swift liquid movement, a twist of the wrist, and he's already plucking the feathers with the other hand, ignoring the death-spasms. And I'm real close now. I can smell him. Mud and sweat. Behind him, the open sea. On the deck, the feathers, a bloody snowfall.

He bites off the head and I hear the skull crunch.

I scream. He whirls. I try to cover it up with a childish giggle.

He speaks in a monotone. Slowly. Sounding out each syllable, but he seems to have picked up a little pidgin. "Little white boy. You go upstairs. No belong here."

"I go where I want. They don't care."

He offers me a raw wing.

"Boy hungry?"

"Man hungry?"

I fish in my pocket, find half a liverwurst sandwich. I hold it out to him. He shakes his head. We both laugh a little. We've both known this hunger that consumes you; the agony of

China is in our bones.

I say, "Me and Mom are going to Siam. On account of my dad getting killed by the Japs and we can't live in Shanghai anymore. We were in a camp and everything." He stares blankly and so I bark in Japanese, like the guards used to. And he goes crazy.

He mutters to himself in Hakka which I don't understand that well, but it's something like, "Don't look 'em in the eye. They chop off your head. You stare at the ground, they leave you alone." He is chewing away at raw bird flesh the whole time. He adds in English, "Si Ui no like Japan man."

"Makes two of us," I say.

I've seen too much. Before the internment camp, there was Nanking. Mom was gonna do an article about the atrocities. I saw them. You think a two-year-old doesn't see anything? She carried me on her back the whole time, papoose-style.

When you've seen a river clogged with corpses, when you've looked at piles of human heads, and human livers roasting on spits, and women raped and set on fire, well, Santa and the Tooth Fairy just don't cut it. I pretended about the Tooth Fairy, though, for a long time. Because, in the camp, the ladies would pool their resources to bribe Mr. Tooth Fairy Sakamoto for a little piece of fish.

"I'm Nicholas," I say.

"Si Ui." I don't know if it's his name or something in Hakka.

I hear my mother calling from the upper deck. I turn from the strange man, the raw bird's blood trailing from his lips. "Gotta go." I turn to him, pointing at my chest, and I say, "Nicholas."

Even the upper deck is cramped. It's hotter than Shanghai, hotter even than the internment camp. We share a cabin with two Catholic priests who let us hide out there after suspecting we didn't have tickets.

Night doesn't get any cooler, and the priests snore. I'm down to a pair of shorts and I still can't sleep. So I slip away. It's easy. Nobody cares. Millions of people have been dying and I'm just some skinny kid on the wrong side of the ocean. Me and my mom have been adrift for as long as I can remember.

The ship groans and clanks. I take the steep metal stairwell down to the coolies' level. I'm wondering about the bird catcher. Down below, the smells are a lot more comforting. The smell of sweat and soy-stained clothing masks the odor of the sea. The charcoal stove is still burning. The old woman is simmering some stew. Maybe something magical ... a bit of snake's blood to revive someone's limp dick ... crushed tiger bones, powdered rhinoceros horn, to heal pretty much anything. People are starving, but you can still get those kind of ingredients. I'm eleven, and I already know too much.

They are sleeping every which way, but it's easy for me to step over them even in the dark. The camp was even more crowded than this, and a misstep could get you hurt. There's a little bit of light from the little clay stove.

I don't know what I'm looking for.

Just to be alone, I guess. I can be more alone in a crowd of Chinese than up there. Mom says things will be better in Siam. I don't know.

I've threaded my way past all of them. And I'm leaning against the railing. There isn't much moonlight. It's probably past midnight but the metal is still hot. There's a warm wind, though, and it dries away my sweat. China's too far away to see, and I can't even imagine Boston anymore.

He pounces.

Leather hands rasp my shoulders. Strong hands. Not big, but I can't squirm out of their grip. The hands twirl me around and I'm looking into Si Ui's eyes. The moonlight is in them. I'm scared. I don't know why, really, all I'd have to do is scream and they'll pull him off me. But I can't get the scream out.

I look into his eyes and I see fire. A burning village. Maybe it's just the opium haze that clings to this deck, making me feel all weird inside, seeing things. And the sounds. I think it must be the whispering of the sea, but it's not, it's voices.   Hungry, you little chink? And those leering, bucktoothed faces. Like comic book Japs. Barking. The fire blazes. And then, abruptly, it dissolves. And there's a kid standing in the smoky ruins.   Me.   And I'm holding out a liverwurst sandwich.   Am I really than skinny, that pathetic?   But the vision fades.   And Si Ui's eyes become empty. Soulless.

"Si Ui catch anything," he says. "See, catch bird, catch boy. All same." And smiles, a curiously captivating smile.

"As long as you don't eat me," I say.

"Si Ui never eat Nicholas," he says. "Nicholas friend."

Friend? In the burning wasteland of China, an angel holding out a liverwurst sandwich?   It makes me smile.   And suddenly angry. The anger hits me so suddenly I don't even have time to figure out what it is. It's the war, the maggots in the millet, the commandant kicking me across the yard, but more than that it's my mom, clinging to her journalist fantasies while I dug for earthworms, letting my dad walk out to his death.   I'm crying and the bird catcher is stroking my cheek, saying, "You no cry now.   Soon go back America. No one cry there."   And it's the first time some has touched me with some kind of tenderness in, in, in, I dunno, since before the invasion. Because mom doesn't hug, she kind of encircles, and her arms are like the bars of a cage.

So, I'm thinking this will be my last glimpse of Si Ui.   It's in the harbor at Klong Toei.   You know, where Anna landed in *The King and I.*   And where Joseph Conrad landed in *Youth.*
So all these coolies, and all these trapped Americans and Europeans, they're all stampeding down the gangplank, with cargo being hoisted, workmen trundling, fleets of those bicycle pedicabs called *samlors*, itinerant merchants with bales of silk and fruits that seem to have hair or claws, and then there's the smell that socks you in the face, gasoline and jasmine

and decay and incense.   Pungent salt squid drying on racks. The ever-present fish sauce, blending with the odor of fresh papaya and pineapple and coconut and human sweat.

And my mother's off and running, with me barely keeping up, chasing after some waxed-mustache British doctor guy with one of those accents you think's a joke until you realize that's really how they talk.

So I'm just carried along by the mob.

"You buy bird, little boy?" I look up. It's a wall of sparrows, each one in a cramped wooden cage. Rows and rows of cages, stacked up from the concrete high as a man, more cages hanging from wires, stuffed into the branch-crooks of a mango tree. I see others buying the birds for a few coins, releasing them into the air.

"Why are they doing that?"

"Good for your karma. Buy bird, set bird free, shorten your suffering in your next life."

"Swell," I say.

Further off, the vendor's boy is

catching them, coaxing them back into cages.   That's got to be wrong, I'm thinking as the boy comes back with ten little cages hanging on each arm.   The birds haven't gotten far.   They can barely fly.   Answering my unspoken thought, the bird seller says, "Oh, we clip wings.   Must make living too, you know."

That's when a hear a sound like the thunder of a thousand wings.   I think I must be dreaming.   I look up.   The crowd has parted.   And there's a skinny little shirtless man standing in the clearing, his arms spread wide like a Jesus statue, only you can barely see a square inch of him because he's all covered in sparrows.   They're perched all over his arms like they're telegraph wires or something, and squatting on his head, and clinging to his baggy homespun shorts with their claws.   And the birds are all chattering at once, drowning out the cacophony of the mob.

Si Ui looks at me.   And in his eyes I see ... bars. Bars of light, maybe. Prison bars.   The man's trying to tell me something. I'm trapped.

The crowd that parted all of sudden comes together and he's gone. I wonder if I'm the only one who saw. I wonder if it's just another aftereffect of the opium that clogged the walkways on the ship.

But it's too late to wonder; my mom has found me, she's got me by the arm and she's yanking me back into the stream of people. And in the next few weeks I don't think about Si Ui at all. Until he shows up, just like that, in a village called Thapsakae.

After the museum, I took Corey to Baskin-Robbins and popped into Starbucks next door for a frappuccino. Visiting the boogieman is a draining thing. I wanted to let him down easy. But Corey didn't want to let go right away.

"Can we take a boat ride or something?" he said. "You know I never get to come to this part of town." It's true. The traffic in Bangkok is so bad that they sell little car toilets so you can go while you're stuck at a red light for an hour. This side of town, Thonburi, the old capital, is a lot more like the past. But no one bothers to come. The traffic, they say, always the traffic.

We left the car by a local pier, hailed a river taxi, just told him to go, anywhere, told him we wanted to ride around. Overpaid him. It served me right for being me, an old white guy in baggy slacks, with a facing-backwards-Yankees-hat-toting blond kid in tow.

When you leave the river behind, there's a network of canals, called klongs, that used to be the arteries and capillaries of the old city. In Bangkok proper, they've all been filled in. But not here. The further from the main waterway we floated, the further back in time. Now the klongs were fragrant with jasmine, with stilted houses rearing up behind thickets of banana and bamboo.   And I was remembering more.

Rain jars by the landing docks ... lizards basking in the sun ... young boys leaping into the water.

"The water was a lot clearer," I told my grandson.   "And the swimmers weren't wearing those little trunks ... they were naked."   Recently, fearing to offend the sensibilities of tourists, the Thai government made a fuss about little boys skinny-dipping along the tourist riverboat routes. But the river is so polluted now, one wonders what difference it makes.

They were bobbing up and down around the boat. Shouting in fractured English.   Wanting a lick of Corey's Baskin-Robbins. When Corey spoke to them in Thai, they swam away. Tourists who speak the language aren't tourists anymore.

"You used to do that, huh, grandpa."

"Yes," I said.

"I like the Sports Club better. The water's clean. And they make a mean chicken sandwich at the poolside bar."

I only went to the sports club once in my life. A week after we landed in Bangkok, a week of sleeping in a pew at a missionary church, a week wringing out the same clothes and ironing them over and over.

"I never thought much of the Sports Club," I said.

"Oh, grandpa, you're such a prole." One of his father's words, I thought, smiling.

"Well, I did grow up in Red China," I said.

"Yeah," he said. "So what was it like, the Sports Club?"

... a little piece of England in the midst of all this tropical stuff. The horse races. Cricket. My mother has a rendezvous with the doctor, the one she's been flirting with on the ship. They have tea and crumpets. They talk about the Bangkok Chinatown riots, and about money. I am reading a battered EC comic that I found in the reading room.

"Well, if you don't mind going native," the doctor says, "there's a clinic, down south a bit; pay wouldn't be much, and you'll have to live with the benighted buggers, but I daresay you'll cope."

"Oh, I'll go native," Mom says, "as long as I can keep writing. I'll do anything for that. I'd give you a blowjob if that's what it takes."

"Heavens," says the doctor. "More tea?"

And so, a month later, we come to a fishing village nestled in the western crook of the Gulf of Siam, and I swear it's paradise. There's a village school taught by monks, and a little clinic where Mom works, dressing wounds, jabbing penicillin into people's buttocks; I think she's working on a novel. That doctor she was flirting with got her this job because she speaks Chinese, and the village is full of Chinese immigrants, smuggled across the sea, looking for some measure of freedom.

Thapsakae ... it rhymes with Tupperware ... it's always warm, but never stifling like in Bangkok ... always a breeze from the unseen sea, shaking the ripe coconuts from the trees ... a town of stilted dwellings, a tiny main street with

storefront rowhouses, fields of neon
green rice as far as the eye can see, lazy
waterbuffalo wallowing, and always the
canals running alongside the half-paved
road, women beating their wet laundry
with rocks in the dawn, boys diving in
the noonday heat ... the second day I'm
there, I meet these kids, Lek and
Sombun.   They're my age.   I can't
understand a word they're saying at
first.   I'm watching them, leaning
against a dragon-glazed rain jar, as they
shuck their school uniforms and leap in.
They're laughing a lot, splashing, one
time they're throwing a catfish back and
forth like it's some kind of volleyball,
but they're like fishes themselves, silvery
brown sleek things chattering in a
singsong language. And I'm alone, like I
was at the camp, flinging stones into the
water.   Except I'm not scared like I was
there.   There's no time I have to be
home.   I can reach into just about any
thicket and pluck out something good
to eat: bananas, mangoes, little pink
sour-apples.   My shorts are all torn (I
still only have one pair) and my shirt is

stained with the juices of exotic fruits, and I let my hair grow as long as I want.

Today I'm thinking of the birds.

You buy a bird to free yourself from the cage of karma. You free the bird, but its wings are clipped and he's inside another cage, a cage circumscribed by the fact that he can't fly far. And the boy that catches him is in another cage, apprenticed to that vendor, unable to fly free. Cages within cages within cages. I've been in a cage before; one time in the camp they hung me up in one in the commandant's office and told me to sing.

Here, I don't feel caged at all.

The Thai kids have noticed me and they pop up from the depths right next to me, staring curiously. They're not hostile. I don't know what they're saying, but I know I'm soon going to absorb this musical language. Meanwhile, they're splashing me, daring me to dive in, and in the end I throw off these filthy clothes and I'm in the water and it's clear and warm and full of fish. And we're laughing and chasing each

other.   And they do know a few words
of English; they've picked it up in that
village school, where the monks have
been ramming a weird antiquated
English phrasebook down their throats.

But later, after we dry off in the sun
and they try to show me how to ride a
waterbuffalo, later we sneak across the
gailan field and I see him again.   The
Bird Catcher, I mean.   Gailan is a
Chinese vegetable like broccoli only
without the bushy part.   The Chinese
immigrants grow it here, They all work
for this one rich Chinese man named
Tae Pak, the one who had the refugees
shipped to this town as cheap labor.

"You want to watch TV?" Sombun
asks me.

I haven't had much of a chance to
see TV.   He takes me by the lead and
pulls me along, with Lek behind him,
giggling.   Night has fallen.   It happens
really suddenly in the tropics, boom and
it's dark.   In the distance, past a wall of
bamboo trees, we see glimmering lights.
Tae Pak has electricity.   Not that many
private homes have.   Mom and I use

kerosene lamps at night.   I've never
been to his house, but I know we're
going there.   Villagers are zeroing in on
the house now, walking surefootedly in
the moonlight.   The stench of night-
blooming jasmine is almost choking in
the compound.   A little shrine to the
Mother of Mercy stands by the entrance,
and ahead we see what passes for a
mansion here; the wooden stilts and the
thatched roof with the pointed eaves,
like everyone else's house, but spread
out over three sides of a quadrangle,
and in the center a ruined pagoda
whose origin no one remembers.

The usual pigs and chickens are
running around in the space under the
house, but the stairway up to the
veranda is packed with people, kids
mostly, and they're all gazing upward.
The object of their devotion is a
television set, the images on it ghostly,
the sound staticky and in Thai in any
case ... but I recognize the show ... it's *I
Love Lucy*.   And I'm just staring and
staring.   Sombun pushes me up the
steps. I barely remember to remove my

sandals and step in the trough at the bottom of the steps to wash the river-mud off my feet.   It's really true. I can't understand a word of it but it's still funny. The kids are laughing along with the laugh track.

Well ... that's when I see Si Ui.   I point at him.   I try to attract his attention, but he too, sitting cross-legged on the veranda, is riveted to the screen.   And when I try to whisper to Sombun that hey, I know this guy, what a weird coincidence, Sombun just whispers back, "Jek, jek," which I know is a putdown word for a Chinaman.

"I know him," I whisper. "He catches birds. And eats them. Alive." I try to attract Si Ui's attention.   But he won't look at me.   He's too busy staring at Lucille Ball. I'm a little bit afraid to look at him directly, scared of what his eyes might disclose, our shared and brutal past.

Lek, whose nickname just means "Tiny", shudders.

"Jek, jek," Sombun says.   The laugh track kicks in.

Everything has changed now that I know he's here. On my reed mat, under the mosquito nets every night, I toss and turn, and I see things. I don't think they're dreams. I think it's like the time I looked into Si Ui's eyes and saw the fire. I see a Chinese boy running through a field of dead people. It's sort of all in black and white and he's screaming and behind him a village is burning.

At first it's the Chinese boy but somehow it's me too, and I'm running, with my bare feet squishing into dead men's bowels, running over a sea of blood and shit. And I run right into someone's arms. Hard. The comic-book Japanese villain face. A human heart, still beating, in his hand.

"Hungry, you little chink?" he says.

Little chink. Little jek.

Intestines are writhing up out of disemboweled bodies like snakes. I saw a lot of disemboweled Japs. Their officers did it in groups, quietly, stony-faced. The honorable thing to do.

I'm screaming myself awake.   And then, from the veranda, maybe, I hear the tap of my mom's battered typewriter, an old Hermes she bought in the Sunday market in Bangkok for a hundred baht.

I crawl out of bed. It's already dawn.

"Hi, Mom," I say, as I breeze past her, an old phakomah wrapped around my loins.

"Wow. It talks."

"Mom, I'm going over to Sombun's house to play."

"You're getting the hang of the place, I take it."

"Yeah."

"Pick up some food, Nicholas."

"Okay."   Around here, a dollar will feed me and her three square meals. But it won't take away the other hunger.

Another lazy day of running myself ragged, gorging on papaya and coconut milk, another day in paradise.

It's time to meet the serpent, I decide.

Sombun tells me someone's been

killed, and we sneak over to the police station. Si Ui is there, sitting at a desk, staring at a wall. I think he's just doing some kind of alien registration thing. He has a Thai interpreter, the same toothless woman I saw on the boat. And a policeman is writing stuff down in a ledger.

There's a woman sitting on a bench, rocking back and forth. She's talking to everyone in sight. Even me and Sombun.

Sombun whispers, "That woman Daeng. Daughter die."

Daeng mumbles, "My daughter. By the railway tracks. All she was doing was running down the street for an ice coffee. Oh, my terrible karma." She collars a passing inspector. "Help me. My daughter. Strangled, raped."

"That inspector Jed," Sombun whispered to me. "Head of the whole place."

Inspector Jed is being polite, compassionate and efficient at the same time. I like him. My mom should hang out with people like that instead of the losers who are just looking for a quick lay.

The woman continues muttering to herself. "Nit, nit, nit, nit, nit," she says. That must be the girl's name. They all have nicknames like that. Nit means "tiny", too, like Lek. "Dead, strangled," she says. "And this town is supposed to be heaven on earth. The sea, the palm trees, the sun always bright. This town has a dark heart."

Suddenly, Si Ui looks up. Stares at her. As though remembering something. Daeng is sobbing. And the policeman who's been interviewing him says, "Watch yourself, chink. Everyone smiles here. Food falls from the trees. If a little girl's murdered, they'll file it away; they won't try to find out who did it. Because this is a perfect place, and no one gets murdered. We all love each other here ... you little jek."

Si UI has this weird look in his eye. Mesmerized. My mother looks that way sometimes ... when a man catches her eye and she's zeroing in for the kill. The woman's mumbling that she's going to go be a nun now, she has nothing left to live for.

"Watch your back, jek," says the policeman. He's trying, I realize, to help this man, who he probably thinks is some kind of village idiot type. "Someone'll murder you just for being a stupid little chink. And no one will bother to find out who did it."

"Si Ui hungry," says Si Ui.

I realize that I speak his language, and my friends do not.

"Si Ui!" I call out to him.

He freezes in his tracks, and slowly turns, and I look into his eyes for the second time, and I know that it was no illusion before.

Somehow we've seen through each other's eyes.

I am a misfit kid in a picture-perfect town with a dark heart, but I understand what he's saying, because though I look all different I come from where he comes from. I've experienced what it's like to be Chinese. You can torture them and kill them by millions, like the Japs did, and still they endure.

They just shake it off. They've outlasted everyone so far. And will till the end of time. Right now in Siam they're the coolies and the laborers, and soon they're going to end up owning the whole country. They endure. I saw their severed heads piled up like battlements, and the river choked with their corpses, and they outlasted it all.

These Thai kids will never understand.

"See Ui hungry!' the man cries.

That afternoon, I slip away from my friends at the river, and I go to the gailan field where I know he works. He never acknowledges my presence, but later, he strides further and further from the house of his rich patron, towards a more densely wooded area past the fields. It's all banana trees, the little bananas that have seeds in them, you chew the whole banana and spit out the seeds, rat-tat-tat, like a machine gun. There's bamboo, too, and the jasmine bushes that grow wild, and mango trees. Si Ui doesn't talk to me, doesn't look back, but somehow I know I'm supposed to follow him.

And I do.

Through the thicket, into a private clearing, the ground overgrown with weeds, the whole thing surrounded by vegetation, and in the middle of it a tumbledown house, the thatch unpatched in places, the stilts decaying and carved with old graffiti. The steps are lined with wooden cages. There's birdshit all over the decking, over the wooden railings, even around the foot trough. Birds are chattering from the cages, from the air around us. The sun has been searing and sweat is running down my face, my chest, soaking my phakhomah.

We don't go up into the house. Instead, Si Ui leads me past it, toward a clump of rubber trees. He doesn't talk, just keeps beckoning me, the curious way they have of beckoning, palm pointing toward the ground.

I feel dizzy. He's standing there. Swaying a little. Then he makes a little clucking, chattering sound, barely opening his lips. The birds are gathering.   He seems to know their language.   They're answering him.   The chirping around us grows to a screeching cacophony.   Above, they're circling.   They're blocking out the sun and it's suddenly chilly.   I'm scared now. But I don't dare say anything.   In the camp, if you said anything, they always hurt you.   Si Ui keeps beckoning me: nearer, come nearer.   And I creep up. The birds are shrieking.   And now they're swooping down, landing, ga- thering at Si Ui's feet, their heads moving to and fro in a regular rhythm, like they're listening to ... a heartbeat. Si Ui's heartbeat.   My own.

An image flashes into my head.   A little Chinese boy hiding in a closet ... listening to footsteps ... breathing nervously.

He's poised.   Like a snake, coiled up, ready to pounce.   And then, without warning, he drops to a crouch, pulls a bird out of the sea of birds, puts it to his lips, snaps its neck with his teeth, and the blood just spurts, all over his bare skin, over the homespun wrapped

around his loins, an impossible crimson.
And he smiles. And throws me the bird.

I recoil. He laughs again when I let
the dead bird slip through my fingers.
Pounces again and gets me another.

"Birds are easy to trap," he says to me
in Chinese, "easy as children, sometimes; you just have to know their
language." He rips one open, pulls out a
slippery liver. "You don't like them raw,
I know," he says, "but come, little
brother, we'll make a fire."

He waves his hand, dismisses the
birds; all at once they're gone and the
air is steaming again. In the heat, we
make a bonfire and grill the birds' livers
over it. He has become, I guess, my
friend. Because he's become all
talkative. "I didn't rape her," he says.

Then he talks about fleeing through
the rice fields. There's a war going on
around him. I guess he's my age in his
story, but in Chinese they don't use past
or future, everything happens in a kind
of abstract now-time. I don't
understand his dialect that well, but
what he says matches the waking

dreams I've had tossing and turning under that mosquito net. There was a Japanese soldier. He seemed kinder than the others. They were roasting something over a fire. He was handing Si Ui a morsel. A piece of liver.

Hungry, little chink?

Hungry. I understand hungry.

Human liver.

In Asia they believe that everything that will ever happen has already happened. Is that what Si Ui is doing with me, forging a karmic chain with his own childhood, the Japanese soldier?

There's so much I want to ask him, but I can't form the thoughts, especially not in Chinese. I'm young, Corey. I'm not thinking karmic cycles. What are you trying to ask me?

"I thought Si Ui ate children's livers," said Corey. "Not some dumb old birds'."

We were still on the klong, turning back now toward civilization; on either side of us were crumbling temples, old houses with pointed eaves, each one with its little totemic spirit house by the front gate, pouring sweet incense into the air, the air itself dripping with humidity. But ahead, just beyond a turn in the klong, a series of eighty-story condos reared up over the banana trees.

"Yes, he did," I said, "and we'll get to that part, in time. Don't be impatient."

"Grandpa, Si Ui ate children's livers. Just like Dracula bit women in the neck. Well like, it's the main part of the story. How long are you gonna make me wait?"

"So you know more than you told me before. About the maid trying to scare you one time, when you were five."

"Well, yeah, grandpa, I saw the miniseries. It never mentioned you."

"I'm part of the secret history, Corey."

"Cool." He contemplated his Pokémon, but decided not to go back to monster trapping. "When we get back to the Bangkok side, can I get another caramel frappuccino at Starbucks?"

"Decaf," I said.

That evening I go back to the house

and find Mom in bed with Jed, the police detective. Suddenly, I don't like Jed anymore.

She barely looks up at me; Jed is pounding away and oblivious to it all; I don't know if Mom really knows I'm there, or just a shadow flitting beyond the mosquito netting. I know why she's doing it; she'll say that it's all about getting information for this great novel she's planning to write, or research for a major magazine article, but the truth is that it's about survival; it's no different from that concentration camp.

I think she finally does realize I'm there; she mouths the words "I'm sorry" and then turns back to her work. At that moment, I hear someone tapping at the entrance, and I crawl over the squeaky floor-planks, Siamese style (children learn to move around on their knees so that their head isn't accidentally higher than someone of higher rank) to see Sombun on the step.

"Can you come out?" he says. "There's a ngaan wat."

I don't know what that is, but I don't

want to stay in the house. So I throw on
a shirt and go with him. I soon find out
that a Ngaan Wat is a temple fair, sort of
a cross between a carnival and a church
bazaar and a theatrical night out.

Even from a mile or two away we
hear the music, the tinkling of
marimbas and the thud of drums, the
wail of the Javanese oboe. By the time
we get there, the air is drenched with
the fragrance of pickled guava, peanut
pork skewers, and green papaya tossed
in fish sauce. A makeshift dance floor
has been spread over the muddy ground
and there are dancers with rhinestone
court costumes and pagoda hats, their
hands bent back at an impossible angle.
There's a Chinese opera troupe like I've
seen in Shanghai, glittering costumes,
masks painted on the faces in garish
colors, boys dressed as monkeys leaping
to and fro; the Thai and the Chinese
striving to outdo each other in noise
and brilliance. And on a grill, being
tended by a fat woman, pigeons are
barbecuing, each one on a mini-spear of
steel. And I'm reminded of the open

fire and the sizzling of half-plucked feathers.

"You got money?" Sombun says. He thinks that all farangs are rich. I fish in my pocket and pull out a few saleungs, and we stuff ourselves with pan-fried roti swimming in sweet condensed milk.

The thick juice is dripping from our lips. This really is paradise. The music, the mingled scents, the warm wind. Then I see Si Ui. There aren't any birds nearby, not unless you count the pigeons charring on the grill. Si Ui is muttering to himself, but I understand Chinese, and he's saying, over and over again, "Si Ui hungry, Si Ui hungry." He says it in a little voice and it's almost like baby talk.

We wander over to the Chinese opera troupe. They're doing something about monkeys invading heaven and stealing the apples of the gods. All these kids are somersaulting, tumbling, cartwheeling, and climbing up onto each other's shoulders. There's a little girl, nine or ten maybe, and she's watching the show. And Si Ui is watching her. And I'm watching him.

I've seen her before, know her from that night we squatted on the veranda staring at American TV shows. Was Si Ui watching her even then? I tried to remember. Couldn't be sure. Her name's Juk.

Those Chinese cymbals, with their annoying "boing-boing-boing" sound, are clashing. A man is intoning in a weird singsong. The monkeys are leaping. Suddenly I see, in Si Ui's face, the same expression I saw on the ship. He's utterly still inside, utterly quiet, beyond feeling. The war did that to him. I know. Just like it made my Mom into a whore, and me into ... I don't know ... a bird without a nesting place ... a lost boy.

And then I get this ... irrational feeling. That the little girl is a bird, chirping to herself, hopping along the ground, not noticing the stalker.

So many people here. So much jangling, so much laughter. The town's dilapidated pagodas sparkle with reflected colors, like stone Christmas trees.   Chinese opera rings in my ears, I look away, when I look back they are gone ... Sombun is preoccupied now, playing with two-saleung top that he just bought. Somehow feel impelled to follow. To stalk the stalker.

I duck behind a fruit stand and then I see a golden deer. It's a toy, on four wheels, pulled along a string. I can't help following it with my eyes as it darts between hampers full of rambutans and pomelos.

The deer darts toward the cupped hands of the little girl. I see her disappear into the crowd, but then I see Si Ui's face too; you can't mistake the cold fire in his eyes.

She follows the toy. Si Ui pulls. I follow, too, not really knowing why it's so fascinating. The toy deer weaves through the ocean of feet. Bare feet of monks and novices, their saffron robes skimming the mud. Feet in rubber flipflops, in the wooden sandals the Jek call kiah. I hear a voice: Juk, Juk! And I know there's someone else looking for the girl, too. It's a weird quartet, each one in the sequence known only to the next one.   I can Si Ui now, his head bobbing up and down in the throng because he's a little taller than the average Thai even though he's so skinny. He's intent. Concentrated. He seems to be on wheels himself, he glides through the crowd like the toy deer does.   The woman's voice, calling for Juk, is faint and distant; she hears it, I'm sure, but she's ignoring her mother or her big sister. I only hear it because my senses are sharp now, it's like the rest of the temple fair's all out of focus now, all blurry, and there's just the four of us. I see the woman now, it must be a mother or aunt, too old for a sister, collaring a roti vendor and asking if he's seen the child.   The vendor shakes his head, laughs. And suddenly we're all next to the pigeon barbecue, and if the woman was only looking in the right place she'd see the little girl, giggling as she clambers through the forest of legs, as the toy zigzags over the dirt aisles. And now the deer has been yanked right up to Si Ui's feet. And the girl crawls all the way after it, seizes it, laughs, looks solemnly up at the face of the Chinaman —

"It's him! It's the chink!" Sombun is pointing, laughing. I'd forgotten he was even with me.

Si Ui is startled. His concentration snaps. He lashes out. There's a blind rage in his eyes. Dead pigeons are flying everywhere.

"Hungry!" he screams in Chinese. "Si Ui hungry!"

He turns. There is a cloth stall nearby. Suddenly he and the girl are gone amid a flurry of billowing sarongs. And I follow.

Incense in the air, stinging my eyes. A shaman gets possessed in a side aisle, his followers hushed. A flash of red. A red sarong, embroidered with gold, a year's wages, twisting through the crowd. I follow. I see the girl's terrified eyes. I see Si Ui with the red cloth wrapped around his arms, around the girl. I see something glistening, a knife maybe. And no one sees. No one but me.

Juk! Juk!

I've lost Sombun somewhere. I don't
care. I thread my way through a bevy of
ramwong dancers, through men dressed
as women and women dressed as men.
Fireworks are going off.   There's an
ancient wall, the temple boundary,
crumbling ... and the trail of red funnels
into black night ... and I'm standing on
the other side of the wall now, watching
Si Ui ride away in a pedicab, into the
night. There's moonlight on him. He's
saying something; even from far off I
can read his lips; he's saying it over and
over: Si Ui hungry, Si Ui hungry.

So they find her by the side of the
road with her internal organs missing.
And I'm there too, all the boys are at
dawn, peering down, daring each other
to touch.   It's not a rape or anything,
they tell us. Nothing like the other girl.
Someone has seen a cowherd near the
site, and he's the one they arrest. He's
an Indian, you see. If there's anyone the
locals despise more than the Chinese,
it's the Indians. They have a saying: if

you see a snake and an Indian, kill the babu.

Later, in the market, Detective Jed is escorting the Indian to the police station, and they start pelting him with stones, and they call him a dirty Indian and a cowshit eater. They beat him up pretty badly in the jail. The country's under martial law in those days, you know. They can beat up anyone they want. Or shoot them.

But most people don't really notice, or care. After all, it is paradise. To say that it is not, aloud, risks making it true. That's why my mom will never belong in Siam; she doesn't understand that everything there resides in what is left unsaid.

That afternoon I go back to the rubber orchard.   He is standing patiently. There's a bird on a branch. Si Ui is poised. Waiting. I think he is about to pounce. But I'm too excited to wait. "The girl," I say. "The girl, she's dead, did you know?"

Si Ui whirls around in a murderous

fury, and then, just as suddenly, he's smiling.

"I didn't mean to break your concentration," I say.

"Girl soft," Si Ui says. "Tender." He laughs a little. I don't see a vicious killer. All I see is loneliness and hunger.

"Did you kill her?" I say.

"Kill?" he says. "I don't know. Si Ui hungry." He beckons me closer. I'm not afraid of him. "Do like me," he says. He crouches. I crouch too. He stares at the bird. And so do I. "Make like a tree now," he says, and I say, "Yes. I'm a tree." He's behind me. He's breathing down my neck. Am I the next bird? But somehow I know he won't hurt me.

"Now!" he shrieks. Blindly, instinctively, I grab the sparrow in both hands. I can feel the quick heart grow cold as the bones crunch. Blood and birdshit squirt into my fists. It feels exciting, you know, down there, inside me. I killed it. The shock of death is amazing, joyous. I wonder if this is what grownups feel when they do things to each other in the night.

He laughs. "You and me," he says, "now we same-same."

He shows me how to lick the warm blood as it spurts. It's hotter than you think. It pulses, it quivers, the whole bird trembles as it yields up its spirit to me.

And then there's the weirdest thing. You know that hunger, the one that's gnawed at me, like a wound that won't close up, since we were dragged to that camp ... it's suddenly gone. In it's place there's a kind of nothing.

The Buddhists here say that heaven itself is a kind of nothing. That the goal of all existence is to become as nothing.

And I feel it. For all of a second or two, I feel it. "I know why you do it," I say. "I won't tell anyone, I swear."

"Si Ui knows that already."

Yes, he does. We have stood on common ground. We have shared communion flesh. Once a month, a Chinese priest used to come to the camp and celebrate mass with a hunk of maggoty man to, but he never made me feel one with anyone, let alone God.

The blood bathes my lips. The liver is succulent and bursting with juices.

Perhaps this is the first person I've ever loved.

The feeling lasts a few minutes. But then comes the hunger, swooping down on me, hunger clawed and ravenous. It will never go away, not completely.

They have called in an exorcist to pray over the railway tracks.   The mother of the girl they found there has become a nun, and she stands on the gravel pathway lamenting her karma. The most recent victim has few to grieve for her. I overhear Detective Jed talking to my mother.   He tells her there are two killers.   The second one had her throat cut and her internal organs removed ... the first one, strangulation, all different ... he's been studying these cases, these ritual killers, in American psychiatry books. And the cowherd has an alibi for the first victim.

I'm only half-listening to Jed, who drones on and on about famous mad killers in Europe.   Like the butcher of

Hanover, Jack the Ripper.   How their victims were always chosen in a special way.   How they killed over and over, always a certain way, a ritual. How they always got careless after a while, because part of what they were doing came from a hunger, a desperate need to be found out. How after a while they might leave clues ... confide in someone ... how he thought he had one of these cases on his hands, but the authorities in Bangkok weren't buying the idea. The village of Thapsakae just wasn't grand enough to play host to a reincarnation of Jack the Ripper.

I listen to him, but I've never been to Europe, and it's all just talk to me. I'm much more interested in the exorcist, who's a Brahmin, in white robes, hair down to his feet, all nappy and filthy, a dozen flower garlands around his neck, and amulets tinkling all over him.

"The killer might confide in someone," says Jed, "someone he thinks is in no position to betray him, someone perhaps too simpleminded to understand. Remember, the killer doesn't know he's evil. In a sense, he really can't help himself. He doesn't think the way we think. To himself, he's an innocent."

The exorcist enters his trance and sways and mumbles in unknown tongues. The villagers don't believe the killer's an innocent. They want to lynch him.

Women washing clothes find a young girl's hand bobbing up and down, and her head a few yards downstream. Women are panicking in the marketplace. They're lynching Indians, Chinese, anyone alien. But not Si Ui; he's a simpleton, after all. The village idiot is immune from persecution because every village needs an idiot.

The exorcist gets quite a workout, capturing spirits into baskets and jars.

Meanwhile, Si Ui has become the trusted Jek, the one who cuts the gailan in the fields and never cheats anyone of their two-saleung bundle of Chinese broccoli.

I keep his secret. Evenings, after I'm exhausted from swimming all day with

Sombun and Lek, or lazing on the back of a waterbuffalo, I go to the rubber orchard and catch birds as the sun sets. I'm almost as good as him now. Sometimes he says nothing, though he'll share with me a piece of meat, cooked or uncooked; sometimes he talks up a storm. When he talks pidgin, he sounds like he's a half-wit. When he talks Thai, it's the same way, I think. But when he goes on and on in his Hakka dialect, he's as lucid as they come. I think. Because I'm only getting it in patches.

One day he says to me, "The young ones taste the best because it's the taste of childhood. You and I, we have no childhood. Only the taste."

A bird flies onto his shoulder, head tilted, chirps a friendly song. Perhaps he will soon be dinner.

Another day, Si Ui says, "Children's livers are the sweetest, they're bursting with young life. I weep for them. They're with me always. They're my friends. Like you."

Around us, paradise is crumbling. Everyone suspects someone else. Fights are breaking out in the marketplace. One day it's the Indians, another day the chinks, the Burmese. Hatred hangs in the air like the smell of rotten mangoes.

And Si Ui is getting hungrier.

My mother is working on her book now, thinking it'll make her fortune; she waits for the mail, which gets here sometimes by train, sometimes by oxcart. She's waiting for some letter from Simon and Schuster. It never comes, but she's having a ball, in her own way. She stumbles her way through the language, commits appalling solecisms, points her feet, even touches a monk one time, a total sacrilege ... but they let her get away with everything. Farangs, after all, are touched by a divine madness. You can expect nothing normal from them.

She questions every villager, pores over every clue. It never occurs to her to ask me what I know.

We glut ourselves on papaya and curried catfish.

"Nicholas," my mother tells me one

evening, after she's offered me a hit of opium, her latest affectation, "this really is the Garden of Eden."

I don't tell her that I've already met the serpent.

Here's how the day of reckoning happened, Corey:

It's mid-morning and I'm wandering aimlessly. My mother has taken the train to Bangkok with detective Jed. He's decided that her untouchable farang-ness might get him an audience with some major official in the police department. I don't see my friends at the river or in the marketplace. But it's not planting season, and there's no school. So I'm playing by myself, but you can only flip so many pebbles into the river, and tease so many water-buffaloes.

After a while I decide to go and look for Sombun. We're not close, he and I, but we're thrown together a lot; things don't seem right without him.

I go to Sombun's house; it's a shabby place, but immaculate, a row house in the more "citified" part of the village, if you can call it that. Sombun's mother is making chili paste, pounding the spices in a stone mortar. You can smell the sweet basil and the lemongrass in the air. And the betelnut, too; she's chewing on the intoxicant; her teeth are stained red-black from long use.

"Oh," she says, "the farang boy."

"Where's Sombun?"

She's doesn't know quite what to make of my Thai, which has been getting better for months. "He's not home, Little Mouse," she says. "He went to the Jek's house to buy broccoli. Do you want to eat?"

"I've eaten, thanks, auntie," I say, but for politeness' sake I'm forced to nibble on bright green sali pastry.

"He's been gone a long time," she said, as she pounded. "I wonder if the chink's going to teach him to catch birds."

"Birds?"

And I start to get this weird feeling. Because I'm the one who catches birds with the Chinaman, I'm the one who's shared his past, who understands his hunger. Not just any kid.

"Sombun told me the chink was going to show him a special trick for catching them. Something about putting yourself into a deep state of samadhi, reaching out with your mind, plucking the life-force with your mind. It sounds very spiritual, doesn't it? I always took the chink for a moron, but maybe I'm misjudging him; Sombun seems to do a much better job," she said. "I never liked it when they came to our village, but they do work hard."

Well, when I leave Sombun's house, I'm starting to get a little mad. It's jealousy, of course, childish jealousy; I see that now. But I don't want to go there and disrupt their little bird-catching session. I'm not a spoilsport. I'm just going to pace up and down by the side of the klong, doing a slow burn.

The serpent came to me! I was the only one who could see through his madness and his pain, the only one who truly knew the hunger that drove him! That's what I'm thinking. And I go back to tossing pebbles, and I tease the gibbon chained by the temple's gate, and I kick a waterbuffalo around. And, before I knew it, this twinge of jealousy has grown into a kind of rage. It's like I was one of those birds, only in a really big cage, and I'd been flying and flying and thinking I was free, and now I've banged into the prison bars for the first time. I'm so mad I could burst.

I'm playing by myself by the railway tracks when I see my mom and the detective walking out of the station. And that's the last straw. I want to hurt someone. I want to hurt my mom for shutting me out and letting strangers into her mosquito net at night. I want to punish Jed for thinking he knows everything. I want someone to notice me.

So that's when I run up to them and I say, "I'm the one! He confided in me! You said he was going to give himself away to someone and it was me, it was me!"

My mom just stares at me, but Jed becomes very quiet. "The Chinaman?"

he asks me.

I say, "He told me children's livers are the sweetest. I think he's after Sombun." I don't tell him that he's only going to teach Sombun to catch birds, that he taught me too, that boys are safe from him because like the detective told us, we're not the special kind of victim he seeks out. "In his house, in the rubber orchard, you'll find everything," I say. "Bones. He makes the feet into a stew," I add, improvising now, because I've never been inside that house. "He cuts off their faces and dries them on a jerky rack. And Sombun's with him."

The truth is, I'm just making trouble. I don't believe there's dried faces in the house or human bones. I know Sombun's going to be safe, that Si Ui's only teaching him how to squeeze the life force from the birds, how to blunt the ancient hunger. Him instead of me. They're not going to find anything but dead birds.

There's a scream. I turn. I see Sombun's mother with a basket of fish, coming from the market. She's overheard me, and she cries, "The chink is killing my son!" Faster than thought, the street is full of people, screaming their anti-chink epithets and pulling out butcher knives.   Jed's calling for reinforcements.   Street vendors are tightening their phakhomas around their waists.

"Which way?" Jed asks, and suddenly I'm at the head of an army, racing full tilt toward the rubber orchard, along the neon green of the young rice paddies, beside the canals teeming with catfish, through thickets of banana trees, around the walls of the old temple, through the fields of gailan ... and this too feeds my hunger.   It's ugly. He's a Chinaman. He's the village idiot. He's different. He's an alien. Anything is possible.

We're converging on the gailan field now. They're waving sticks. Harvesting sickles. Fishknives. They're shouting, "Kill the chink, kill the chink."   Sombun's mother is shrieking and wailing, and Detective Jed has his gun out. Tae Pak, the village rich man, is vainly trying to stop the mob from trampling his broccoli. The army is unstoppable. And I'm their leader, I brought them here with my little lie. Even my mother is finally in awe.

I push through the bamboo thicket and we're standing in the clearing in the rubber orchard now. They're screaming for the Jek's blood. And I'm screaming with them.

Si Ui is nowhere to be found. They're beating on the ground now, slicing it with their scythes, smashing their clubs against the trees. Sombun's mother is hysterical. The other women have caught her mood, and they're all screaming now, because someone is holding up a sandal ... Sombun's.

... a little Chinese boy hiding in a closet ...

The images flashes again. I must go up into the house. I steal away, sneak up the steps, respectfully removing my sandals at the veranda, and I slip into the house.

A kerosene lamp burns. Light and shadows dance. There is a low wooden platform for a bed, a mosquito net, a woven rush mat for sleeping; off in a corner, there is a closet.

Birds everywhere.   Dead birds pinned to the walls.   Birds' heads piled up on plates.   Blood spatters on the floorplanks.   Feathers wafting.   On a charcoal stove in one corner, there's a wok with some hot oil and garlic, and sizzling in that oil is a heart, too big to be the heart of a bird....

My eyes get used to the darkness. I see human bones in a pail. I see a young girl's head in a jar, the skull sawn open, half the brain gone.   I see a bowl of pickled eyes.

I'm not afraid.   These are familiar sights. This horror is a spectral echo of Nanking, nothing more.

"Si Ui," I whisper. "I lied to them. I know you didn't do anything to Sombun. You're one of the killers who does the same thing over and over. You don't eat boys. I know I've always been safe with you. I've always trusted you."

I hear someone crying. The whimper of a child.

"Hungry," says the voice. "Hungry."

A voice from behind the closet door.

...

The door opens.   Si Ui is there, huddled, bone-thin, his phakomah about his loins, weeping, rocking.

Noises now. Angry voices. They're clambering up the steps.   They're breaking down the wall planks. Light streams in.

"I'm sorry," I whisper.   I see fire flicker in his eyes, then drain away as the mob sweeps into the room.

My grandson was hungry, too. When he said he could eat the world, he wasn't kidding. After the second decaf frappuccino, there was Italian ice in the Oriental's coffee shop, and then, riding back on the Skytrain to join the chauffeur who had conveniently parked at the Sogo mall, there was a box of Smarties. Corey's mother always told me to watch the sugar, and she had plenty of Ritalin in stock — no prescription needed here — but it was always my pleasure to defy my daughter-in-law and leave her to deal with the consequences.

Corey ran wild in the skytrain station, whooping up the staircases, yelling at old ladies. No one minded. Kids are indulged in Babylon East; little blond boys are too cute to do wrong. For some, this noisy, polluted, chaotic city is still a kind of paradise.

My day of revelations ended at my son's townhouse in Sukhumvit, where maids and nannies fussed over little Corey and undressed him and got him in his Pokémon pajamas as I drained a glass of Beaujolais. My son was rarely home; the taco chain consumed all his time. My daughter-in-law was a social butterfly; she had already gone out for the evening, all pearls and Thai silk. So it fell to me to go into my grandson's room and to kiss him goodnight and goodbye.

Corey's bedroom was little piece of America, with its Phantom Menace drapes and its Playstation. But on a high niche, an image of the Buddha looked down; a decaying garland still perfumed the air with a   whiff of jasmine.   The air conditioning was chilly; the Bangkok of the rich is a cold city; the more conspicuous the consumption, the lower the thermostat setting.   I shivered, even as I missed Manhattan in January.

"Tell me a story, grandpa?" Corey said.

"I told you one already," I said.

"Yeah, you did," he said wistfully. "About you in the Garden of Eden, and the serpent who was really a kid-eating monster."

All true.   But as the years passed I had come to see that perhaps I was the serpent.   I was the one who mixed lies with the truth, and took away his innocence.   He was a child, really, a hungry child.   And so was I.

"Tell me what happened to him," Corey said.   "Did the people lynch him?"

"No.   The court ruled that he was a madman, and sentenced him to a mental home.   But the military government of Field Marshal Sarit reversed the decision, and they took him away and shot him. And he didn't even kill half the kids they said he killed."

"Like the first girl, the one who was raped and strangled," Corey said, "but she didn't get eaten. Maybe that other killer's still around." So he had been paying attention after all. I know he loves me, though he rarely says so; he had suffered an old man's ramblings for one long air conditioning-free day, without complaint. I'm proud of him, can barely believe I've held on to life long enough to get to know him.

I leaned down to kiss him. He clung to me; and, as he let go, he asked me sleepily, "Do you ever feel that hungry, grandpa?"

I didn't want to answer him; so, without another word, I slipped quietly away.

That night, I wandered in my dreams through fields of the dead; the hunger raged; I killed, I swallowed children whole and spat them out; I burned down cities; I stood aflame in my self-made inferno, howling with elemental grief; and in the morning, without leaving a note, I took a taxi to the airport and flew back to New York.

To face the hunger.

Bonus Story

CHUI CHAI

The living dead are not as you imagine them. There are no dangling innards, no dripping slime. They carry their guts and gore inside them, as do you and I. In the right light they can be beautiful, as when they stand in a doorway caught between cross-shafts of contrasting neon. Fueled by the right fantasy, they become indistinguishable from us. Listen. I know. I've touched them.

In the 80s I used to go to Bangkok a lot. The brokerage I worked for had a lot of business there, some of it shady, some not. The flight of money from Hong Kong had begun and our company, vulture that it was, was staking out its share of the loot. Bangkok was booming like there was no tomorrow. It made Los Angeles seem like Peoria. It was wild and fast and frantic and frustrating. It had temples and buildings shaped like giant robots. Its skyline was a cross between Shangri-La and Manhattan. For a dapper yuppie executive like me there were always meetings to be taken, faxes to fax, traffic to be sat in, credit cards to burn. There was also sex.

There was Patpong.

I was addicted. Days, after hours of high-level talks and poring over papers and banquets that lasted from the close of business until midnight, I stalked the crammed alleys of Patpong. The night smelled of sewage and jasmine. The heat seeped into everything. Each step I took was colored by a different neon sign.   From half-open nightclub doorways buttocks bounced to jaunty soulless synthrock. Everything was for sale; the women, the boys, the pirated software, the fake Rolexes. Everything sweated.   I stalked the streets and sometimes at random took an entrance, took in a live show, women propelling ping-pong balls from their pussies, boys buttfucking on motorbikes.   I was addicted.   There were other entrances where I sat in waiting rooms, watched women with numbers around their necks through the one-way glass, soft, slender brown women.   Picked a number.   Fingered the American-made condoms in my pocket. Never buy the local ones, brother, they leak like a sieve.

I was addicted. I didn't know what I was looking for. But I knew it wasn't something you could find in Encino.   I was a knight on a quest, but I didn't know that to find the holy grail is the worst thing that can possibly happen.

I first got a glimpse of the grail at Club Pagoda, which was near my hotel and which is where we often liked to take our clients. The club was on the very edge of Patpong, but it was respectable — the kind of place the serves up a plastic imitation of *The King and I,* which is, of course, a plastic imitation of life in ancient Siam ... artifice imitating artifice, you see. Waiters crawled around in Mediaeval uniforms, the guests sat on the floor, except there was a well under the table to accommodate the dangling legs of lumbering white people. The floor show was eminently sober ... it was all classical Thai dances, women wearing those pagoda-shaped hats moving with painstaking grace and slowness to a tinkling, alien music. A good place to interview prospective grant recipients, because it tended to make them very nervous.

Dr. Frances Stone wasn't at all nervous though. She was already there when I arrived. She was preoccupied with picking the peanuts out of her *gaeng massaman* and arranging them over her rice plate in such a way that they looked like little eyes, a nose, and a mouth.

"You like to play with your food?" I said, taking my shoes off at the edge of our private booth and sliding my legs under the table across from her.

"No," she said, "I just prefer them crushed rather than whole. The peanuts I mean. You must be Mr. Leibowitz."

"Russell."

"The man I'm supposed to charm out of a few million dollars." She was doing a sort of coquettish pout, not really the sort of thing I expected from someone in medical research. Her face was ravaged, but the way she smiled kindled the memory of youthful beauty. I wondered what had happened to change her so much; according to her dossier, she was only in her mid-forties.

"Mostly we're in town to take," I said, "not to give. R&D is not one of our

strengths.   You might want to go to
Hoechst or Berli Jucker, Frances."

"But Russell...."   She had not
touched her curry, but the peanuts on
the rice were now formed into a perfect
human face, with a few strands of sauce
for hair. "This is not exactly R&D. This
is a discovery that's been around for
almost a century and a half. My great-
grandfather's paper—"

"For which he was booted out of the
Austrian Academy? Yes, my dossier is
pretty thorough, Dr. Stone; I know all
about how he fled to America and
changed his name."

She smiled. "And my dossier on
you, Mr. Leibowitz, is pretty thorough
too," she said, as she began removing a
number of compromising photographs
from her purse.

A gong sounded to announce the
next dance. It was a solo. Fog roiled
across the stage, and from it a woman
emerged.   Her clothes glittered with
crystal beadwork, but her eyes outshone
the yards of cubic zirconia. She looked

at me and I felt the pangs of the addiction.   She smiled and her lips seemed to glisten with lubricious moisture.

"You like what you see," Frances said softly.

"I —"

"The dance is called *Chui Chai,* the dance of transformation. In every Thai classical drama, there are transformations — a woman transforming herself into a rose, a spirit transforming itself into a human. After the character's metamorphosis, he performs a *Chui Chai* dance, exulting in the completeness and beauty of his transformed self."

I wasn't interested, but for some reason she insisted on giving me the entire story behind the dance. "This particular *Chui Chai* is called *Chui Chai Benjakai* ... the demoness Benjakai has been despatched by the demon king, Thotsakanth, to seduce the hero Rama ... disguised as the beautiful Sita, she will float down the river toward Rama's camp, trying to convince him that his beloved has died ... only when she is placed on a funeral pyre, woken from her deathtrance by the flames, will she take on her demonic shape once more and fly away toward the dark kingdom of Lanka. But you're not listening."

How could I listen? She was the kind of woman that existed only in dreams, in poems. Slowly she moved against the tawdry backdrop, a faded painting of a palace with pointed eaves. Her feet barely touched the floor. Her arms undulated. And always her eyes held me. As though she were looking at me alone. Thai women can do things with their eyes that no other women can do. Their eyes have a secret language.

"Why are you looking at her so much?" said Frances. "She's just a Patpong bar girl ... she moonlights here ... classics in the evening, pussy after midnight."

"You know her?" I said.

"I have had some ... dealings with her."

"Just what is it that you're doing research into, Dr. Stone?"

"The boundary between life and death," she said. She pointed to the photographs. Next to them was a contract, an R&D grant agreement of some kind. The print was blurry. "Oh, don't worry, it's only a couple of million dollars ... your company won't even miss it ... and you'll own the greatest secret of all ... the tree of life and death ... the apples of Eve. Besides, I know your price and I can meet it." And she looked at the dancing girl. "Her name is Keo. I don't mind procuring if it's in the name of science."

Suddenly I realized that Dr. Stone and I were the only customers in the Club Pagoda. Somehow I had been set up.

The woman continued to dance, faster now, her hands sweeping through the air in mysterious gestures. She never stopped looking at me. She *was* the character she was playing, seductive and diabolical. There was darkness in every look, every hand-movement.   I downed the rest of my Kloster lager and beckoned for another.   An erection strained against my pants.

The dance ended and she prostrated herself before the audience of two, pressing her palms together in a graceful *wai*.   Her eyes downcast, she left the stage.   I had signed the grant papers without even knowing it.

Dr. Stone said, "On your way to the upstairs toilet ... take the second door on the left. She'll be waiting for you."

I drank another beer, and when I looked up she was gone.   She hadn't eaten one bite.   But the food on her plate had been sculpted into the face of a beautiful woman.   It was so lifelike that ... but no. It wasn't alive. It wasn't breathing.

She was still in her dancing clothes when I went in.   A little girl was carefully taking out the stitches with a seamripper.   There was a pile of garments on the floor. In the glare of a naked bulb, the vestments of the goddess had little glamor. "They no have buttons on classical dance clothes," she said. "They just sew us into them. Cannot go pipi!" She giggled.

The little girl scooped up the pile and slipped away.

"You're ... very beautiful," I said. "I don't understand why ... I mean, why you *need* to...."

"I have problem," she said. "Expensive problem. Dr. Stone no tell you?"

"No." Her hands were coyly clasped across her bosom. Gently I pried them away.

"You want I dance for you?"

"Dance," I said. She was naked. The way she smelled was different from other women. It was like crushed flowers. Maybe a hint of decay in them. She shook her hair and it coiled across her breasts like a nest of black serpents. When I'd seen her on stage I'd been entertaining some kind of rape fantasy about her, but now I wanted to string it out for as long as I could. God, she was driving me mad.

"I see big emptiness inside you. Come to me. I fill you. We both empty people. Need filling up."

I started to protest. But I knew she had seen me for what I was.   I had money coming out my ass, but I was one fucked up yuppie. That was the root of my addiction.

Again she danced the dance of transforming, this time for me alone. Really for me alone. I mean, all the girls in Patpong have this way of making you think they love you. It's what gets you addicted.   It's the only street in the world where you *can* buy love. But that's not how she was.   When she touched me it was as though she reached out to me across an invisible barrier, an unbreachable gulf.   Even when I entered her she was untouchable.   We were from different worlds and neither of us ever left our private hells.

Not that there wasn't passion. She knew every position in the book. She knew them backwards and forwards. She kept me there all night and each act seemed as though it been freshly invented for the two of us. It was the last time I came that I felt I had glimpsed the grail. Her eyes, staring up into the naked bulb, brimmed with some remembered sadness. I loved her with all my might. Then I was seized with terror. She was a demon. Yellow-eyed, dragon-clawed. She was me, she was my insatiable hunger. I was fucking my own addiction. I think I sobbed. I accused her of lacing my drink with hallucinogens. I cried myself to sleep and then she left me.

I didn't notice the lumpy mattress or the peeling walls or the way the light bulb jiggled to the music from downstairs. I didn't notice the cockroaches.

I didn't notice until morning that I had forgotten to use my condoms.

It was a productive trip but I didn't go back to Thailand for another two years. I was promoted off the traveling circuit, moved from Encino to Beverly Hills, got myself a newer, late-model wife, packed my kids off to a Swiss boarding school. I also found a new therapist and a new support group. I smothered the addiction in new addictions. My old therapist had been a strict Freudian. He'd tried to root out the cause from some childhood trauma — molestation, potty training, Oedipal games — he'd never been able to find anything. I'm good at blocking out memories. To the best of my knowledge, I popped into being around age eight or nine. My parents were dead but I had a trust fund.

My best friends in the support group were Janine, who'd had eight husbands, and Mike, a transvestite with a spectacular fro. The clinic was in Malibu so we could do the beach in between bouts of tearing ourselves apart. One day Thailand came up.

Mike said, "I knew this woman in Thailand. I had fun in Thailand, you know? R&R. Lot of transvestites there, hon. I'm not a fag, I just like lingerie. I met this girl." He rarely stuck to the point because he was always stoned. Our therapist, Glenda, had passed out in the redwood tub. The beach was deserted. "I knew this girl in Thailand, a dancer. She would change when she danced. I mean *change*. You shoulda seen her skin. Translucent. And she smelled different. Smelled of strange drugs."

You know I started shaking when he said that because I'd tried not to think of her all this time even though she came to me in dreams. Even before I'd start to dream, when I'd just closed my eyes, I'd hear the hollow tinkle of marimbas and see her eyes floating in the darkness.

"Sounds familiar," I said.

"Nah. There was nobody like this girl, hon, nobody. She danced in a classical dance show *and* she worked the whorehouses ... had a day job too, working for a nutty professor woman ... honky woman, withered face, glasses. Some kind of doctor, I think. Sleazy office in Patpong, gave the girls free V.D. drugs."

"Dr. Frances Stone." Was the company paying for a free V.D. clinic? What about the research into the secrets of the universe?

"Hey, how'd you know her name?"

"Did you have sex with her?" Suddenly I was trembling with rage. I don't know why. I mean, I knew what she did for a living.

"Did you?" Mike said. He was all nervous. He inched away from me, rolling a joint with one hand and scootching along the redwood deck with the other.

"I asked first," I shouted, thinking, Jesus, I sound like a ten-year-old kid.

"Of *course* not! She had problems, all right? Expensive problems. But she was beautiful, mm-mm, good enough to eat."

I looked wildly around.   Mr. Therapist was still dozing — fabulous way to earn a thousand bucks an hour — and the others had broken up into little groups.   Janine was sort of listening, but she was more interested in getting her suntan lotion on evenly.

"I want to go back," I said. "I want to see Keo again."

"Totally, like, bullshit," she said, sidling up to me. "You're just, like, externalizing the interior hurt onto a fantasy-object. Like, you need to be in touch with your child, know what I mean?"

"You're getting your support groups muddled up, hon," Mike said edgily.

"Hey, Russ, instead of, like, projecting on some past-forgettable female two years back and ten thousand miles away, why don't you, like, fixate on someone a little closer to home? I mean, I've been *looking* at you. I only joined this support group cause like, support groups are the only place you can find like *sensitive* guys."

"Janine, I'm married."

"So let's have an affair."

I liked the idea. My marriage to Trisha had mostly been a joke; I'd needed a fresh ornament for cocktail parties and openings; she needed security. We hadn't had much sex; how could we? I was hooked on memory. Perhaps this woman would cure me. And I wanted to be cured so badly because Mike's story had jolted me out of the fantasy that Keo had existed only for me.

By now it was the 90s so Janine insisted on a blood test before we did anything. I tested positive. I was scared shitless. Because the only time I'd ever been so careless as to forget to use a condom was ... that night. And we'd done everything. Plumbed every orifice. Shared every fluid.

It had been a dance of trans-formation all right.

I had nothing to lose. I divorced my wife and sent my kids to an even more expensive school in Connecticut. I was feeling fine. Maybe I'd never come down with anything. I read all the books and articles about it. I didn't tell anyone. I packed a couple of suits and some casual clothes and a supply of bootleg AZT. I was feeling fine. Fine, I told myself. Fine.

I took the next flight to Bangkok.

The company was surprised to see me, but I was such a big executive by now they assumed I was doing some kind of internal troubleshooting. They put me up at the Oriental. They game me a 10,000 baht per diem. In Bangkok you can buy a lot for four hundred bucks. I told them to leave me alone. The investigation didn't concern them. They didn't know what I was investigating, so they feared the worst.

I went to Silom Road, where Club Pagoda had stood. It was gone. In its stead stood a brand new McDonalds and an airline ticket office. Perhaps Keo was already dead. Wasn't that what I had smelled on her? The odor or crushed flowers, wilting ... the smell of coming death?   And the passion with which she had made love. I understood it now.   It was the passion of the damned.   She had reached out to me from a place between life and death. She had sucked the life from me and given me the virus as a gift of love.

I   strolled   through Patpong. Hustlers tugged at my elbows.   Fake Rolexes were flashed in my face. It was useless to ask for Keo.   There are a million women named Keo.   Keo means jewel. It also means glass. In Thai there are many words that are used indiscriminately for reality and artifice. I didn't have a photograph and Keo's beauty was hard to describe. And every girl in Patpong is beautiful. Every night, parading before me in the neon labyrinth, a thousand pairs of lips and eyes, sensuous and infinitely giving. The wrong lips, the wrong eyes.

There are only a few city blocks in Patpong, but to trudge up and down them in the searing heat, questioning, observing every face for a trace of the remembered grail ... it can age you. I stopped shaving and took recreational drugs. What did it matter anyway?

But I was still fine, I wasn't coming down with anything.

I was fine. Fine!

And then, one day, while paying for a Big Mac, I saw her hands. I was looking down at the counter counting out the money. I heard the computer beep of the cash register and then I saw them: proffering the hamburger in both hands, palms up, like an offering to the gods. The fingers arched upwards, just so, with delicacy and hidden strength. God, I knew those hands. Their delicacy as they skimmed my shoulder blades, as they glided across my testicles just a hair's breadth away from touching. Their strength when she balled up her fist and shoved it into my rectum. Jesus, we'd done everything that night. I dropped my wallet on the counter, I seized those hands and gripped them, burger and all, and I felt the familiar response. Oh, God, I ached.

"Mister, you want a blowjob?"

It wasn't her voice. I looked up. It wasn't even a woman.

I looked back down at the hands. I looked up at the face. They didn't even belong together. It was a pockmarked boy and when he talked to me he stared off into space.   There was no relation between the vacuity of his expression and the passion with which those hands caressed my hands.

"I don't like to do such thing," he said, "but I'm a poor college student and I needing money. So you can come back after 5 p.m. You not be disappointed."

The fingers kneaded my wrists with the familiarity of one who has touched every part of your body, who has memorized the varicose veins in your left leg and the mole on your right testicle.

It was obscene. I wrenched my own hands free.   I barely remembered to retrieve my wallet before I ran out into the street.

I had been trying to find Dr. Frances Stone since I arrived, looking through the files at the corporate headquarters, screaming at secretaries. Although the corporation had funded Dr. Stone's project, the records seemed to have been spirited away.

At last I realized that that was the wrong way to go about it. I remembered what Mike had told me, so the day after the encounter with Keo's hands, I was back in Patpong, asking around for a good V.D. clinic. The most highly regarded one of all turned out to be at the corner of Patpong and Soi Cowboy, above a store that sold pirated software and videotapes.

I walked up a steep staircase into a tiny room without windows, with a ceiling fan moving the same sweaty air around and around. A receptionist smiled at me. Her eyes had the same vacuity that the boy at McDonalds had possessed. I sat in an unraveling rattan chair and waited, and Dr. Stone summoned me into her office.

"You've done something with her," I said.

"Yes." She was shuffling a stack of papers. She had a window; she had an airconditioner blasting away in the direction of all the computers. I was still drenched with sweat.

The phone rang and she had a brief conversation in Thai that I couldn't catch. "You're angry, of course," she said, putting down the phone. "But it was better than nothing. Better than the cold emptiness of the earth. And she had nothing to lose."

"She was dying of AIDS! And now *I* have it!" It was the first time I'd allowed the word to cross my lips. "You *killed* me!"

Frances laughed. "My," she said, "aren't we being a little melodramatic? You have the virus, but you haven't actually come down with anything."

"I'm fine. Fine."

"Well, why don't you sit down. I'll order up some food. We'll talk."

She had really gone native. In Thailand it's rude to talk business without ordering up food. Sullenly I sat down while she opened a window and yelled out an order to one of the street vendors.

"To be honest, Mr. Leibowitz," she said, "we really could use another grant. We had to spend *so* much of the last one on cloak-and-dagger nonsense, security, bribes, and so on; so little could be spared for research itself ... I mean, look around you ... I'm not exactly wasting money on luxurious office space, am I?"

"I saw her hands."

"Very effective, wasn't it?" The food arrived. It was some kind of noodle thing wrapped in banana leaves and groaning from the weight of chili peppers. She did not eat; instead, she amused herself by rearranging the peppers in the shape of ... "The hands, I mean. Beautiful as ever. Vibrant. Sensual. My first breakthrough."

I started shaking again. I'd read about Dr. Stone's great-grandfather and his graverobbing experiments. Jigsaw corpses brought to life with bolts of lightning. Not life. A simulacrum of life. Could this have happened to Keo? But she was dying. Perhaps it was better than nothing. Perhaps....

"Anyhow. I was hoping you'd arrive soon, Mr. Leibowitz. Because we've made up another grant proposal. I have the papers here. I know that you've become so important now that your signature alone will suffice to bring us ten times the amount you authorized two years ago."

"I want to see her."

"Would you like to dance with her? Would you like to see her in the *Chui Chai* one more time?"

She led me down a different stairwell. Many flights. I was sure we were below ground level. I knew we were getting nearer to Keo because there was a hint of that rotting flower fragrance in the air. We descended. There was an unnatural chill.

And then, at last, we reached the laboratory. No shambling Igors or bubbling retorts. Just a clean, well-lit basement room. Cold, like the vault of a morgue. Walls of white tile; ceiling of stucco; fluorescent lamps; the pervasive smell of the not-quite-dead.

Perspex tanks lined the walls. They were full of fluid and body parts. Arms and legs floating past me. Torsos twirled. A woman's breast peered from between a child's thighs. In another tank, human hearts swirled, each neatly severed at the aorta. There was a tank of eyes. Another of genitalia. A necklace of tongues hung suspended in a third. A mass of intestines writhed in a fourth. Computers drew intricate charts on a bank of monitors. Oscilloscopes beeped. A pet gibbon was chained to a post topped by a human skull. There was something so outlandishly antiseptic about this spectacle that I couldn't feel the horror.

"I'm sorry about the décor, Russell, but you see, we've had to forgo the usual decoration allowance." The one attempt at dressing up the place was a frayed poster of *Young Frankenstein* tacked to the far wall. "Please don't be upset at all the body parts," she added. "It's all very macabre, but one gets inured to it in med school; if you feel like losing your lunch, there's a small restroom on your left ... yes, between the eyes and the tongues." I did not feel sick. I was feeling ... excited. It was the odor. I knew I was getting closer to Keo.

She unlocked another door. We stepped into an inner room.

Keo was there. A cloth was draped over her, but seeing her face after all these years made my heart almost stop beating. The eyes. The parted lips. The hair, streaming upward toward a source of blue light ... although I felt no wind in the room. "It is an electron wind," said Dr. Stone. "No more waiting for the monsoon lightning.   We can get more power from a wall socket than great-grandfather Victor could ever dream of stealing from the sky."

And she laughed the laughter of mad scientists.

I saw the boy from McDonalds sitting in a chair.   The hands reached out toward me.   There were electrodes fastened to his temples.   He was naked now, and I saw the scars where the hands had been joined at the wrists to someone else's arms.   I saw a woman with Keo's breasts, wired to a pillar of glass, straining, heaving while jags of blue lightning danced about her bonds. I saw her vagina stitched onto the pubis of a dwarf, who lay twitching at the foot of the pillar.   Her feet were fastened to the body of a five-year-old boy, transforming their grace to ungainliness as he stomped in circles around the pillar.

"Jigsaw people!" I said.

"Of course!" said Dr. Stone.   "Do you think I would be so foolish as to

bring back people whole? Do you not
realize what the consequences would
be? The legal redefinition of life and
death ... wills declared void, humans
made subservient to walking corpses ...
I'm a scientist, not a philosopher."

"But who are they now?"

"They were nobody before. Street
kids. Prostitutes. They were dying, Mr.
Leibowitz, dying! They were glad to will
their bodies to me. And now they're
more than human. They're many
persons in many bodies. A gestalt. I
can shuffle them and put them back
together, oh, so many different ways ...
and the beautiful Keo. Oh, she wept
when she came to me. When she found
out she had given you the virus. She
loved you. You were the last person she
ever loved. I saved her for you. She's
been sleeping here, waiting to dance for
you, since the day she died. Oh, let us
not say *died*. The day she ... she ... I am
no poet, Mr. Leibowitz. Just a scientist."

I didn't want to listen to her. All I
could see was Keo's face. It all came

back to me. Everything we had done. I wanted to relive it. I didn't care if she was dead or undead. I wanted to seize the grail and clutch it in my hands and own it.

Frances threw a switch. The music started. The shrilling of the *pinai,* the pounding of the *taphon,* the tinkling of marimbas and xylophones rang in the *Chui Chai* music. Then she slipped away unobtrusively. I heard a key turn in a lock. She had left the grant contract lying on the floor. I was alone with all the parts of the woman I'd loved. Slowly I walked toward the draped head. The electron wind surged; the cold blue light intensified. Her eyes opened. Her lips moved as though discovering speech for the first time....

"Rus ... sell."

On the pizzafaced boy, the hands stirred of their own accord. He turned his head from side to side and the hands groped the air, straining to touch my face. Keo's lips were dry. I put my arms around the drape-shrouded body and kissed the dead mouth. I could feel my hair stand on end.

"I see big emptiness inside you. Come to me. I fill you. We both empty people. Need filling up."

"Yes. Jesus, yes."

I hugged her to me.   What I embraced was cold and prickly.   I whisked away the drape. There was no body. Only a framework of wires and transistors and circuit boards and tubes that fed flasks of flaming reagents.

"I dance for you now."

I turned.   The hands of the McDonalds boy twisted into graceful patterns. The feet of the child moved in syncopation to the music, dragging the rest of the body with them. The breasts of the chained woman stood firm, waiting for my touch. The music welled up.   A contralto voice spun plaintive melismas over the interlocking rhythms of wood and metal. I kissed her. I kissed that severed head and lent my warmth to the cold tongue, awakened passion in her. I kissed her. I could hear chains breaking and wires slithering along the floortiles. There were hands pressed into my spine, rubbing my neck, unfastening my belt. A breast touched my left buttock and a foot trod lightly on my right. I didn't care that these parts were attached to other bodies. They were hers. She was loving me all over. The dwarf that wore her pudenda was climbing up my leg. Every part of her was in love with me. Oh, she danced. We danced together. I was the epicenter of their passion. We were empty people but now we drank our fill. Oh, God, we danced. Oh, it was a grave music, but it contented us.

And I signed everything, even the codicil.

Today I am in the AIDS ward of a Beverly Hills hospital. I don't have long to wait. Soon the codicil will come into effect, and my body will be preserved in liquid nitrogen and shipped to Patpong.

The nurses hate to look at me. They come at me with rubber gloves on so I won't contaminate them, even though they should know better. My insurance policy has disowned me. My children no longer write me letters, though I've paid for them to go to Ivy League colleges. Trisha comes by sometimes. She is happy that we rarely made love.

One day I will close my eyes and wake up in a dozen other bodies. I will be closer to her than I could ever be in life. In life we are all islands. Only in Dr. Stone's laboratory can we know true intimacy, the mind of one commanding the muscles of another and causing the nerves of a third to tingle with un-nameable desires. I hope I shall die soon.

The living dead are not as you imagine them. There are no dangling innards, no dripping slime. They carry their guts and gore inside them, as do you and I. In the right light they can be beautiful, as when they stand in the cold luminescence of a basement laboratory, waiting for an electron stream to lend them the illusion of life.   Fueled by the right fantasy, they become indistinguishable from us.

Listen. I know. I've loved them.

About the Author

Once referred to by the *International Herald Tribune* as "the most well-known expatriate Thai in the world," Somtow Sucharitkul is no longer an expatriate, since he has returned to Thailand after five decades of wandering the world. He is best known as an award-winning novelist and a composer of operas.

Born in Bangkok, Somtow grew up in Europe and was educated at Eton and Cambridge. His first career was in music and in the 1970s he acquired a reputation as a revolutionary composer, the first to combine Thai and Western instruments in radical new sonorities. Conditions in the arts in the region at the time proved so traumatic for the young composer that he suffered a major burnout, emigrated to the United States, and reinvented himself as a novelist.

His earliest novels were in the science fiction field but he soon began to cross into other genres. In his 1984 novel Vampire Junction, he injected a new literary inventiveness into the horror genre, in the words of Robert Bloch, author of Psycho, "skillfully combining the styles of Stephen King, William Burroughs, and the author of the Revelation to John." *Vampire Junction* was voted one of the forty all-time greatest horror books by the Horror Writers' Association, joining established classics like *Frankenstein* and *Dracula*.

In the 1990s Somtow became increasingly identified as a uniquely Asian writer with novels such as the semi-autobiographical *Jasmine Nights.* He won the World Fantasy Award, the highest accolade given in the world of fantastic literature, for his novella *The Bird Catcher.* His fifty-three books have sold about two million copies worldwide.

After becoming a Buddhist monk for a period in 2001, Somtow decided to refocus his attention on the country of his birth, founding Bangkok's first international opera company and returning to music, where he again reinvented himself, this time as a neo-Asian neo-Romantic composer. The Norwegian government commissioned his song cycle *Songs Before Dawn* for the 100th Anniversary of the Nobel Peace Prize, and he composed at the request of the government of Thailand his *Requiem: In Memoriam 9/11* which was dedicated to the victims of the 9/11 tragedy.

According to London's Opera magazine, "in just five years, Somtow has made Bangkok into the operatic hub of Southeast Asia." His operas on Thai themes, *Madana, Mae Naak,* and

Ayodhya, have been well received by international critics. His most recent opera, *The Silent Prince,* was premiered in 2010 in Houston, and a fifth opera, *Dan no Ura,* premiered in Thailand in the 2013 season. Since then, he has composed five more operas, and is embarking on a ten opera cycle, *DasJati - Ten Lives of the Buddha,* which if completed will be the "biggest" single work in the history of performing arts.

He is increasingly in demand as a conductor specializing in opera and in the late-romantic composers like Mahler. His repertoire runs the entire gamut from Monteverdi to Wagner. His work has been especially lauded for its stylistic authenticity and its lyricism. The orchestra he founded in Bangkok, the Siam Philharmonic, has mounted the first complete Mahler cycle in the region.

He is the first recipient of Thailand's "Distinguished Silpathorn" award, given for an artist who has made and continues to make a major impact on the region's culture, from Thailand's Ministry of Culture.

Books by S.P. Somtow

General Fiction
The Shattered Horse
Jasmine Nights
Forgetting Places
The Other City of Angels (Bluebeard's Castle)
The Stone Buddha's Tears

Dark Fantasy
The Timmy Valentine Series:
    Vampire Junction
    Valentine
    Vanitas
Vampire Junction Special Edition
Moon Dance
Darker Angels
The Vampire's Beautiful Daughter

Science Fiction
Starship & Haiku

Mallworld
The Ultimate Mallworld
*The Ultimate, Ultimate, Ultimate
Mallworld*
Chronicles of the High Inquest:
    Light on the Sound
    The Darkling Wind
    The Throne of Madness
    Utopia Hunters
Chroniques de l'Inquisition - Volume 1
(omnibus)
Chroniques de l'Inquisition - Volume 2
(omnibus)

The Aquiliad Series:
    Aquila in the New World
    Aquila and the Iron Horse
    Aquila and the Sphinx

Fantasy
The Riverrun Trilogy:
    Riverrun
    Armorica
    Yestern
The Riverrun Trilogy (omnibus)

The Fallen Country
Wizard's Apprentice
The Snow Dragon (omnibus)

Media Tie-in
The Alien Swordmaster
Symphony of Terror
The Crow - Temple of Night
Star Trek: Do Comets Dream?

Chapbooks
Fiddling for Waterbuffaloes
*I Wake from a Dream of a Drowned Star
City*
A Lap Dance with the Lobster Lady
Compassion — Two Perspectives
The Bird Catcher

Libretti
Mae Naak
Ayodhya
Madana
The Silent Prince
Dan no Ura

Helena Citronova
The Snow Dragon
Sama - The Faithful Son
Nemiraj - The Chariot of Heaven
Mahosadha - The Architect of Dreams

Collections

My Cold Mad Father (in press)
Fire from the Wine Dark Sea
Chui Chai (Thai)
Nova (Thai)
The Pavilion of Frozen Women
Dragon's Fin Soup
Tagging the Moon
Face of Death (Thai)
Other Edens
S.P. Somtow's The Great Tales (Thai)
Terror Nova (in press)
Terror Antiqua (in press)

Essays, Poetry and Miscellanies

Opus Fifty
A Certain Slant of "I" (in press)
Sonnets about Serial Killers

Opera East
Victory in Vienna (ed.)
Three Continents (ed.)
Nirvana Express
Caravaggio x 2
The Maestro's Noctuary

Printed in Great Britain
by Amazon